James Samuel Trout

Life, Adventures and Anecdotes of Beau Hickman

The Prince of American Bummers

James Samuel Trout

Life, Adventures and Anecdotes of Beau Hickman
The Prince of American Bummers

ISBN/EAN: 9783337170660

Printed in Europe, USA, Canada, Australia, Japan

Cover: Foto ©Raphael Reischuk / pixelio.de

More available books at **www.hansebooks.com**

1876 JUST PUBLISHED. 1876

LIFE,

Adventures and Anecdotes

OF

BEAU HICKMAN,

The Prince of American Bummers.

WASHINGTON:

CUNNINGHAM & BRASHEARS, PRINTERS,

1876.

FOR SALE AT THE BOOKSTORES.

PREFACE.

Perhaps an apology should be offered for imposing these sketches of a useless life upon the public. Indeed biographies should never be written of persons who, during their lives, neglected to make memoranda, or failed to preserve any data to insure exact truthfulness. In this instance the writer has had nothing of the kind to aid him, for the subject of these sketches was a professional man of leisure, and eschewed trouble and inconvenience. The main sources to draw from were the *on dit* of the town and general recollections of the country. The files of the *National Republican,* *Washington Chronicle, Evening Star* and the *Capital* also furnished many of the incidents contained in the following pages.

It is hoped that the same excuse that justified the public generally in tolerating and patronizing so singular a character will serve as an apology for thus collecting the main incidents of his life.

THE AUTHOR.

WASHINGTON, D. C., *June* 12, 1876.

LIFE,

ADVENTURES AND ANECDOTES

OF

BEAU HICKMAN.

▶ ◆ ◀

Rarely will it ever occur in any profession that two men will so singularly monopolize the characteristics of a special genius to a greater extent than was the case with George Brummell, the renowned Beau of England, and Robert S. Hickman, the equally famous Beau and Prince of American Bummers. That their's was a profession, as they unblushingly claimed, their life-long practices, and the marvelous success in the accomplishment of their purposes fully establish; and the multifarious creations of plot and scheme exhibit a genius, as well as their executive ability in developing their practices attests a talent of no ordinary character, which, if it had been employed in more legitimate pursuits would most probably have developed equally renowned results. But, as it was, their lives proved signal failures, and the genius and talent of these singular men having been directed solely to the accomplishment of selfish purposes, the world still moves on no better for their having lived, unless, perhaps, the memory of their idiosyncracies may recur

"To point a moral or adorn a tale."

There is a much closer parallel between the general characters of Hickman and Brummell than is, in a casual study, usually conceded. Like Brummell, our American Beau boasted a gentility that was rendered most ludicrously ungenteel in the manner of its practice, and won for them their respective well merited pseudonyms. Both were of respectable parentage—Brummell maintaining a proportionate rank in an aristocratical, to that of Hickman in a republican society. In education they were about equal, neither attaining any degree of proficiency. Where the one boasted the exquisiteness of his toilet and elegance of manners, polished in the drawing rooms of a monarchial aristocracy, the other prided himself in having been brought up in the half feudal, half democratic mannerism of his native State. When, in their early and less disreputable days, the one may have excelled in courtly etiquette and the social intrigues of the drawing-room and club, the other surpassed in the sports of the field and chase, and won the admiration of his associates by his courteous manners, rollicksome humor and careless indifference to the conventionalities of his social sphere. Both were the protegés of generous patrons, and each preferred a life of prodigal gentility sustained by an ungrateful abuse of gratuities. In their declining years fickle fortune respected the great similitude of character and rewarded their unmeritorious lives with bitter penury and want, whilst they languished the miserable remnants of their useless lives, suffering a just mortification at the failure of the experiment of a questionable profession.

But neither should be judged wholly by the catastrophe of their lives, for there was unquestionably with both a phase of character so novel that its ultimate failure to produce beneficial results cannot entirely deprive it of interest. In the heyday of their glory, when they were féted and applauded for the originality of their profession, they won a species of admiration for their genius that developed their unlimited wealth of resource, which must have been as gratifying as the mortification at their ultimate failures was poignant. They can only be properly studied in connection with their times, and it would be unjust to regard them only from the standpoint of their failures, and deprive their history of the eclät of their success. Their great failure was in living too long; and the common judgment must be that the great mistake of their lives was in not directing their talents in the more legitimate professions; and where they did not succeed in acquiring reputation for good, they, as well, avoided a criminal notoriety. There was, however, this difference in the circumstances of the two men—the one had the titled and wealthy for his patrons, and was spared the humility of petty mendaciousness which the other was often forced to practice in a democratic society with less opulent patrons. Had Hickman been thus equally circumstanced he would have been less of the mendacious **Bummer** and more of the genteel Beau, and a more charitable appointment in God's acre would have been allowed, and, it is to be hoped, decency had not been so desecrated as was so outrageously perpetrated on his last humble resting place in Potter's Field.

Robert S. Hickman, who became so familiarly known as Colonel Beau Hickman, was a native of Virginia, born in the year 1813, of respectable parentage. He had been early placed at school, but, although of a quick and sprightly turn of mind, yet he relied mainly upon practices of conciliation to maintain his rank in his classes, and secured the esteem of his mates by a courteous deportment and insinuating confidences. He very readily adopted the current idea that a Virginia gentleman was the ideal of chivalry, and his mannerism the *sine qua non* of gentility. He was early indulged in the social pastimes and amusements that yet savored of the old time manorial customs; and, by his elegant manners and splendid person and jovial disposition he became a general favorite, which preference ultimately proved the means of changing the entire tenor of his after life. About the time when he had obtained his majority and was seriously contemplating adopting some legitimate pursuit, the great catastrophe occurred that hastened his sudden advent out upon the world. His friends had been frequently annoyed by rumors of his tendency towards social conviviality, and even, in several instances, he was suspected of libertinism, and was frequently reprimanded on account of his licentious conduct in the neighborhood. But, unfortunately, these sage counsels were disregarded, and he was finally detected in some disreputable excesses, and, in order to escape the scandal of his follies, he received the share of his patrimony and started from his home and friends a prodigal wanderer, without any defined object or aim in life. About what amount of money he received as his share of the paternal inheritance is not definitely known, but is generally thought to have been about ten thousand dollars, which he very dexterously managed to run through with in a little less than two years in riotous and sumptuous living.

As the practice of the profession of Hickman was regarded by his friends and relatives, who very justly prided themselves upon their social connections, as being so disreputable, it is deemed prudent to omit whatever might refer directly to them, and connect them in any manner with the subject of these sketches. The Beau, himself, scrupulously refrained during his entire life from making any such exposure, and even in the latter days of his faded glory, when poverty assailed him most severely and drove him to his sorest straits, he maintained this confidence, even at the sacrifice of his once vaunted gentility, which, perhaps, may be regarded as the crowning virtue of his life. He allowed no one to question him upon the circumstance of his leaving home, and any such attempt would be promptly met by a sullen rebuke. On one occasion, during the rebellion, an old acquaintance of his one day remarked to him with the kindliest intentions, " Beau, why do you not write down to your old home and find out something about your family. The armies have, no doubt, ravaged that part of the country, and I should think you would feel anxious to know whether your friends are still living, and learn to how great an extent they have been injured by the casualties of war." " Sir," said the deeply offended Beau, drawir himself up to the dignified stature he was so wont on occasions to assume, "you will please to content yourself by minding your own business, and never presume to interfere with mine." So deeply did he resent this imagined insult that he never again spoke to the interrogator.

His first appearance in Washington was in 1833 or 1834, when he was a young man of about twenty or twenty-one years of age. This was in the good old days of the republic, before sectionalism had engendered such deadly antipathies; when Washington was the gay metropolis of representative aristocracy, and the statesman and sportsman and beauty and chivalry held high carnival during the brief sessional terms, and gentility had not yet coined the flunky term of shoddy, when this young gentleman, a stranger and wanderer from his home and friends, first stepped out upon the social boards, where he afterwards won for himself, as Beau and Bummer, a renown as famous as those statesmen of his day who indulged the humor of his bummings, or socially enjoyed the nonchalance of his grotesque gentility.

He immediately plunged into the social cauldron, affected those places of resort and amusement where he would most likely be associated with the representative and sporting classes, and announced himself a sporting character.

He regularly attended and patronized the races, and was always the observed of all observers upon the grounds, and won quite a reputation for his excellent judgment and knowledge of horse-flesh. He became a regular *habitué* of the club, and soon boasted an intimate acquaintance with some of the most eminent statesmen and renowned sporting men of the day; and by his faultless habit and easy and dignified grace of person he was by no means unattractive to the fair denizens of the drawing-room. He dressed in the most approved elegance of the mode, wore a diamond pin, a gold watch and massive fob, carried a cane and wore a faultless beaver, the color and style of which afterwards became so characteristic of the individual. As a gentleman of elegant leisure and fashion his *tout ensémble* was proverbial for neatness, elegance and simplicity.

His money easily purchased him admittance into the most fashionable society, and being fond of a good story, which he could relate with fine effect, he became the life of the club and entertainer at the convivial gatherings of that class of wealthy gentlemen whom he met in their annual visits to the Capital. He was a fine conversationalist, and was frequently invited to evening sociables where were in attendance some of the most noted men of the day, and by his genial humor and courteous deportment won their good opinion, that was never entirely withdrawn from him in his failing fortunes.

He had now fully determined upon a life of easy idleness, and so abandoned had he become to careless prodigality that, in a few years, he found that he had wasted his substance and had become a beggard bankrupt. But he was still constant to his purpose, and when he found he had no longer the means of living upon equal terms with his former companions, he determined to adopt a sort of vagabond Bohemian life, which he chose to distinguish and dignity by the title of profession, and thus secure an idle ease and the comforts of life which he was too proud to work for and too honest to feloniously appropriate.

Thus overleaping the barrier of a legitimate gentility, the late affluent and dashing young Virginian soon became familiarly known as the incorrigible Beau and Bummer; and in a few years had become so notorious that few strangers ever came to Washington without asking to be shown this accomplished character, being perfectly willing to submit to the inevitable tax incident upon every such introduction.

He possessed a remarkable memory of faces and names, and knew all the public men of his time, and, on their annual return to the Capital during the winter season, he would meet them very familiarly and address each by name. He was often tolerated by some of the first statesmen, who would enjoy his jokes and dodges, and often introduced him to their friends from the States, frequently as Colonel Hickman, and then retire to watch the manner in which he would wring from them the price of his acquaintance.

His annual revenue amounted to a very considerable sum, for he lived for many years in good style, and during the summer season he seldom failed to visit one or more of the fashionable watering places, and rarely missed a horse race, for he considered himself *au fait* in all matters pertaining to the turf, and in his latter days could tell of the famous horses of the past thirty years. He was also fond of relating to strangers reminiscenses of great men, and always spoke of them in the most familiar manner.

Perhaps the best method of defining his particular traits of character and idiosyncrasies of talent, as shown in his particular profession, would be to illustrate them by the practical developments of his plots and schemes. Many of his *dodges* have become traditional American jokes, and will be preserved for years to come along with the *anti bellum* traditions of Washington society and famous American celebrities.

HOW HE BEGAN HIS PROFESSION.

After running through with his fortune, and being

suddenly "let down" to a strait of impecuniosity, his turf friends, and other sporting acquaintances, did not desert him, but generously contributed to his support, until, by his natural talent and ingenious address, he became the recognized ward of the traveling public. With this assistance he still adhered to his former mode of living, retaining his preference at the clubs, and preserving his wonted prestige at the races and other places of sport and pastime. Although, after his heavy losses by injudicious bettings, he had determined to refrain from investing in these hazardous sports, yet, so greatly was his opinion in regard to horses esteemed, that he was invariably solicited for his judgment by sporting men, and he made it a source of considerable revenue by accepting liberal gratuities for his advice on matters relating to the races.

His effective manner of story-telling was another method of acquiring a reward; for there was always a wealthy class of gentlemen residing at the Capital who were wont to indulge him in his accomplished "beatings" for the amusement he afforded.

He could readily adapt himself to the different classes of society with which he chanced to be thrown, and in his early days, not then being considered a bore, he found his victims ready and anxious to pay tribute to his eccentricities.

Usually, at the conclusion of a story, he would remark that it was worth a quarter or some other small sum of money, and the listener would laugh and unsuspectingly reply, " Certainly it is—it is a d—d good yarn," but not suspecting the drift of his dodge, would not think of offering the reward, whereupon Beau would say, " Please then pass over the 'chips.'" The victim would be seized with blank amazement, and look quizically at the " Colonel" as he paid over the conceded value of the story, only to be startled by the loud burst of laughter from his friends, who were conveniently posted to enjoy Beau's nonchalance and the victim's innocent amazement.

He was, also, very attentive to strangers, and could very readily insinuate himself into their confidence, and then offer to conduct them to the various places of amusement and interest in the city. He would avail himself of these opportunities to practice his various dodges upon them, and often met with the most unexpected success.

HIS ADVICE ABOUT FARO.

Whenever any of the young gentlemen accompanied him around the city desired visiting gambling-houses, he would very paternally admonish them of their folly, but if they persisted in entering these places, he usually gave them some good advice. He has been charged by some as having been employed as runner or ringer-in to these establishments, but we think from the tenor of his usual advice that the charge was unfounded in fact. "You want to tackle faro, do you?" he would say. "Well, then, let me give you some advice, for I should know something about it. When you get in you will find many players, big and risky ones too. You play light—the dealer may get mad as h—l when he discovers how you play, but never mind him, for he will be compelled to let you win whilst he goes for the heavy players. If you have good luck don't be too greedy, and determine to break the bank, but leave before your luck turns against you." He would generally conclude his cautionary advice by informing his anxious tyro that he usually charged a "red chip" for this advice, which he generally handed into the banker to be cashed. In speaking of money he would usually designate it as "chips," (from the checks used in the game of faro,) the white chips one, the red chips five, and the blue chips representing twenty dollars. He was greatly addicted to the use of professional and technical words and phrases, which, in his later life, became characteristic of his conversation.

ROW HE CHANGED HIS BOARDING.

After he became short in finances, and had let some months pass without settling his board bills as formerly, Mr. Brown, of Brown's Hotel, (now known as the Metropolitan), which place Beau honored with his patronage, informed him finally that his bills were not paid as presented, and that, perhaps, he had just as well step across the way to the National, and share his patronage with that house. "All right, Mr. Brown," cheerfully responded Beau, and forthwith proceeded to the National, where he ordered the best rooms in the house, and, to his astonishment, he was permitted to remain several months before his bills were presented.

This unusual indulgence was occasioned by the mistake of a visitor who mistook Beau for a General Hickman of Kentucky, and the proprietor hearing him addressed as Genl. H., (a mistaken identity which Beau was very innocent of correcting,) and knowing him to be reputed very wealthy, he was unwilling to disturb his opulent guest with the usual monthly statement of account.

HOW BEAU BEAT THE TAILORS.

For a number of years Beau managed to provide that his exchequer should be able to meet any demands that should be made for the purpose of supplying any deficiency in his personal attire. But at last he had run the gamut of his fortune, and he became in sad want of proper habiliments to sustain his fashionable gentility. Becoming reduced to the sorest straits, he determined upon a bold rencounter with the tailors. In the most patronizing manner he would enter their establishments and select materials of the most elegant and costly patterns and order them made up in the latest styles of the fashion, and when the bills were presented for payment Beau would express his great regret at his present impecuniosity, and would have recourse to some clever dodge to stay off the payment until the merchant would gradually realize the true character of his customer; as, for instance, in one case he with imperturable confidence remarked to one of his creditors that " his friend, President Jackson, who by the way, was a d——d good fellow, no matter what some folks might say about him, had borrowed a thousand dollars of him last night, and it would really be impossible to pay that little bill just then." The tailor overawed at the fact that his debtor numbered the President among his intimate friends, was only too glad to conciliate his customer by being very profuse in his apologies and solicitations to use his own convenience in the matter—which time he ultimately learned never occurred to the fashionable Beau, for he seemed to have a conviction of the Shaksperean adage: "Base is the slave that pays." At other times he would solicit fashionable suits, and argue with the tailors that the fact of its becoming generally known that they were the manufacturers of his clothing they would secure the patronage of the fashionable society, who affected his style, and in several instances was successful in thus procuring new out-fits.

HOW HE DID OTHELLO.

There are many little anecdotes in circulation about Beau that cannot be entirely vouched for, among which the following incident is sometimes related. In his early life, when he was yet the reputable gentle-man of elegant leisure, he no doubt made pretension to some gallantry to the fair sex, and it is said he at one time contemplated matrimony. By his splendid address he had attracted the attention of a beautiful southern belle who was spending the winter at the Capital, and had followed his successful suit almost to an engagement. It was his wont to direct his evening walks in the neighborhood where his fair enamorata resided, in order to obtain the opportunity of showing his devotion by little acts of gallantry, and to indulge his vanity in exhibiting his easy manner of bowing, which he could perform in the most elegant style. Washington was then little more than a good sized town planted in a marsh, and utterly innocent of finely paved avenues and streets, and the present sites of the beautiful parks were then only utilized for goat pastures, which species of lacteal quadrupeds were then greatly effected in the suburban districts. Strange as it may seem Beau's matrimonial aspirations were thwarted by an ungainly billy-goat, and his after-life made barren of sentimentality. The story runs, that on one of these occasions, whilst strolling in the vicinity of the residence of "ye fair ladie," he discovered her at her boudoir window, no doubt admiring the fascinating person of the gallant young exquisite; and just as he had struck the *pose* and the *poise,* and was pantomiming his most exquisite bow by bending his person in the form of a crescent, a huge billy-goat, that had become the terror of the neighborhood on account of his bellicose disposition, made a dart from the rear and struck poor Beau in his profundity with such force that he was sent bounding to the front in the most comical gyrations, and finally landed in the acrobatic pose of standing upon his head in his supurb white beaver hat. The situation was too ludicrous for the host of street arabs that crowded around the poor unfortunate, who added mortification and insult to the injuries received by the hideous uproar of their merriment. Sad, dejected, tattered and soiled, the discomfited lover sought his hotel to repair the damage to his clothes and person, and, when in a few days the story of his misfortune leaked out, his companions of the club so irritated him by their ridiculous representations of the scene, that he vowed never again to assume the role of lover. So deep, indeed, was the wound to his vanity that he never recovered from its laceration, and his confidence in his effective gallantry was so greatly impaired that he abandoned every thought of amorous sentimentality.

On one occasion Mr. Clay twitted him on his adventure with the billy-goat, and raised quite a laugh at his expense. Beau endured the ridicule of the great statesman with great composure, but silently determined to have an appropriate revenge in some manner.

Several days after this little pleasantry, Mr. Clay was walking out, as was his usual custom of evenings, with a corner of his red bandanna hanging out of his coat-tail pocket. He happened to pass in the neighborhood of Beau's late adventure, when the same billy-goat espied the red handkerchief and at once made the onset. Mr. Clay performed a very undignified gyration, and recovered himself just in time to intercept the goat on his second expedition after a soft place on his person. Then stood the great statesman holding the goat by the horns, whilst he eagerly interrogated a crowd of hurrahing urchins around him as to the best method of escaping from the goat. "Let go and shin it," advised one of the forward arabs; but the great compromiser effected a bargain with one of the more mercenary of the crowd, whereby it was arranged that the boys were to hold the goat whilst the statesman made good his escape.

Beau heard of this adventure of the gentleman from Kentucky, and bided his time until he met him in the lobby of the hotel with his friends and colleagues, when he told the circumstance of his adventure with the goat, and completely turned the laugh upon his late persecutor, and it is said he doubled his "assessment," with the understanding that Beau was not to further expose his "compromise" with the boys and the goat.

HOW HE OBSERVED PROMISES.

Truthfulness was always a peculiar feature in the character of Beau Hickman. Even in his earlier years he would rather endure the ridicule of his companions than shield himself from his peccadilloes by a denial of their commitment; and up to the day of his death he was known not to be addicted to untruthfulness or promise-breaking, though often sorely tempted by the stress of adverse circumstances. Whatever may have been his peculiarities of habit, they were rather idiosyncrasies than faults. Although he was a cheat upon society, yet he never defrauded through false pretenses ; for he was never known to promise or make an obligation to pay when he practiced his *dodges*, and it is a well known fact that when necessity drove him to legitimate dealing he always liquidated his obligations fairly and satisfactorily. The restaurateurs accounted him a fair customer when he gave his orders in the regular way, as they certainly expected him to put some one else in for the bills when in company with others. It seems that it had become an irresistable mania for him to play his clever *dodges*, for at times, when in affluent circumstances, he was prodigal in the extreme ; yet, for the minor necessities and luxuries he would become the accomplished " *beat*," apparently more for the satisfaction derived from his successes than the enjoyment of the object obtained. This peculiar trait of scrupulous obligation in keeping a promise, never so rashly made, is finally illustrated in his bargain with Colonel T——, then a rising young lawyer of Washington. The Colonel, like all newcomers had, of necessity at that time, to undergo the ordeal of an " introduction" to Col. Hickman, and like all others thus favored, he was compelled to " chip up" to the accomplished celebrity. It was also Beau's habit of following up these introductions with frequent " assessments or

" installments," as he termed it, of his acquaintance-ship. These assessments had been frequently levied upon Col. T——, at short intervals, until, becoming tired of the game, he determined to put a stop to them by the following method :

One day, as the Colonel was walking up the avenue, Beau accosted him and demanded his " installment," when the Colonel informed him that he was getting tired of these " assessments," and requested Beau to walk with him to his rooms, where he would propose a compromise. Beau quite indifferently replied that he would accompany him, and at least hear his prop-osition, but would not yield the point of assessment When they had arrived at the Colonel's rooms, he took from his wardrobe a very fine suit of clothing and pre-sented it to Beau with the understanding that he was *never* to speak to him again under any circumstances. Beau tried on the suit, and after admiring his im-proved appearance in the mirror, he in a very busi-ness-like manner informed the Colonel that he would accede to the proposition, and politely bowed himself out of the apartment. They both lived in Washing-ton for thirty years after this bargain, and scarcely a day passed that he and Beau did not meet on the streets or places of public resort, but Beau passed him by unnoticed as though they had never met, and went on through the gradations of his decline and fall, and at last closed his eyes in his eternal sleep without even breaking this promise. There was no enmity, no harsh feelings toward each other—merely a *promise* that was not to be broken.

HOW HIS NAME WAS USED.

Beau generally was very sensitive and would become highly indignant at any disrespectful allusion to his general character; but at times he would be facetious in his rebuke to what he regarded unwarrantable liberties. On one occasion an acquaintance who was not entirely devoid of some ancient superstitions, and wishing to invest in a lottery, was induced to do so in Beau's name, for the reason that he had heard that if a ticket was held in the name of some worthless or vagabond character it would be insured successful. Let the virtue in superstition be what it may, the ticket really drew one hundred and sixty dollars. Although Beau knew nothing of the transaction, yet the sense of honesty prevailed, and the lucky drawee tendered and paid eighty dollars, one-half of the amount drawn, over to Beau as his share, and informed him of the motive and result of his investment. "Well, that is d——d cool for you, and cheeky as a brass monkey, but hereafter let there be no partnership business between us," Beau cooly retorted, whilst pocketing the "chips."

HOW HE PLAYED ON SOME YOUNG VIRGINIANS.

As was some times the custom with the young men of the neighboring city of Alexandria, a party of four, taking advantage of a fall of snow, started on a sleighing excursion to the Capital, and when they arrived there they drove up at one of the first-class saloons on Pennsylvania avenue. Having entered, and just as the drinks for the party had been ordered, a well dressed gentleman, apparently passed middle age, entered the saloon and stood very indifferently at the counter of the bar, as though he was modestly waiting until the bar-tender was through helping the party of young gentlemen, when, apparently inadvertently, he pretended to have noticed some casual remark of one of the party, and in the very blandest manner imaginable he apologized and begged to know if the gentleman was not a Virginian—as he was lead to infer from a certain remark that he happened incidentally to hear. The gentleman assuring him of the correctness of his inference, he expressed his pleasure by very graciously assuring the gentleman that he himself was proud to boast the same nativity—when he was interrupted by the young Virginian, who replied, that he was always happy to meet with Virginians, and the party pressed the stranger to join them in drinking. "Oh no, my dear friend I could not think of thus imposing myself upon your little party, although I just stepped in to take a little *smile* myself; you will please excuse me, young gentlemen, as I feel the embarrassment of seemingly obtruding." All of which was done in the most patronizing manner. But the party could not think of excusing so polished and affable a Virginia gentleman, whom the bar-tender had just introduced to the party as Col. Hickman, and whom they never for one moment suspected as being the accomplished Beau. "What do you drink, Colonel," was the persistent invitation of the party, until, at last, the over-pressed Colonel very naively suggested that the bar-tender was familiar with his style of drink, and pleasantly nodded his assent to be served. After drinking each other's health, and a friendly interchange of compliments, the Colonel, frequently looking at his watch as if a little impatient, at last remarked: "Well, gentlemen, I thought to take a little luncheon; won't you join me?" "No, no," remarked one of the party; "we came in to have a hot supper, and our distinguished Virginian must be guest to us—no, no; you are at our mercy now."

" Well, well, young gentlemen—I know very well how it is with young Virginians, but really you must excuse me; I cannot consent to so impose upon your liberality." " But you must," interposed one of the party who, perhaps, was mindful of cultivating an influence in Washington, with a selfish idea for political preferment, "you must consent to sup with us— waiter take our orders." " Well, well, really gentlemen, you have the pressing manners of real Virginians—I am heartily glad of having met with you. I hope I shall have the pleasure of a more intimate acquaintance hereafter." After enjoying the supper, he was again pressed to join in the social glass—his being what, as before suggested, the bar-tender knew—when he very politely excused himself to meet another engagement. But when the bill was called for they then suspected the character of their friend's drinks from the surprising item of their cost; for he had too fine an opportunity to indulge in the luxury of imported beverages. Just as he passed out of the saloon, the young gentlemen were startled by a sudden roar of laughter from a far corner of the room, where sat a party of elderly gentlemen unnoticed before by the festive Virginians, and whom they suddenly recognized as intimate acquaintances. "What on earth are you all laughing at?" inquired one of the young party. "Laughing at you, you young fools, to let Beau Hickman *beat* you so unmercifully, and then make you feel so obliged to him for his patronizing assurance." "Beau Hickman," exclaimed the party in wounded surprise, as the truth of the situation flashed upon them. "Come, boys, let us go," suggested one of the dupes, and let us try to study up some plan to estop those confounded spies from telling this on us at home; for if they do we shall never hear the last of how Beau Hickman played the courteous Virginian over us.

HOW HE LEVIED ASSESSMENTS.

Beau's intimacy with many of the first men of his day was greater than was generally suspected, and was often their companion in "bouts" around the city—the zest of their dissipations often drawn from the resources of his fertile genius. Some of their escapades might not have harmonized with their wonted dignities, but they furnished Beau with opportunities for cultivating social familiarities which he was not slow to turn to account.

Beau's habit was to assess the various members of Congress and other officials around Washington with a regular and specific amount, which he would collect in the most business-like manner. At first they would humor his demands on account of his brazen effrontery, which he regarded as a virtual recognition of the demand.

About once every quarter he would present his "bills for quarterage;" nor could the ingenuity of his victims devise any plan to escape the rapaciousness of his demands. His knowledge of human nature was of great service in suggesting the proper time and place for presenting his "bills," which would generally be at some public place when the pseudo debtor was surrounded by colleagues and friends, whilst engaged in good humored hilarity. At one time not to be "patronized" by Beau was considered a slight, and to refuse to humor his "beatings" was thought to be wanting in liberality.

Sometimes his victims would pretend to protest against his frequent "assessments" or complain of excessive charges. On one occasion he met a wealthy southern member and in his proverbially courteous manner intimated that his "quarterage" was in arrear and handed him a slip of paper on which was the statement of his assessment regularly made out. The member objected to the bill as excessive, and proposed a compromise by paying half of the amount. But Beau was unyielding in his demand, and assuming the dignity of a legitimate dealer refused any compromise in the matter. "No, sir," he would. very arrogantly reply, "your assessment is strictly in proportion to

your means; and, sir, knowing that I am no d——d
Hebrew you should not expect me to compromise
myself by entertaining such unbusiness-like proposi-
tions.   Why, sir, if I reduce the ratio of your assessment, that d——d stickler from the other side of the
House would refuse to pay one cent."   Such unscrupulous effrontery would entirely disarm the amused
victim, and he would again pay up his dues, and Beau
would again be enabled to lay in the necessary supplies
for another quarter.

HOW HE ASSUMED THE INDIGNANT.

On one occasion whilst on a visit to Philadelphia he
became very much embarrassed in his finances, and
was put to some sore straits to procure his meals.
Being one day rather severely pressed by his appetite,
he determined on a bold scheme.   He entered a first-
class basement saloon and loitered around, carelessly
observing the pictures on the walls until he heard some
one descending the stairs, when he hastily opened the
door and hurriedly started up the same steps and rudely
collided with a young midshipman of the United States
Navy. . Beau was the first to recover, and very indignantly threw the blame of carelessness upon the
young middy, in thus insulting a gentleman. The young
midshipman was easily convinced by the positive manner

of Beau that he had rudely jostled a gentleman, and was profuse as he was courteous in his apologies, and would insist upon Beau dining with him, when they also drank to the hope that they might remain constant friends. Beau followed the hint, and for some days was a constant visitor to the young midshipman's rooms, and, as it always happened, his calls were made just before the usual meal-times, Beau was invariably prevailed upon to accompany his new found friend, and cultivated his hospitality.

It was some years after, when on a visit to Washington, he happened to meet Beau at one of the hotels, that he found out for the first time that the friend he had made in Philadelphia was the inimitable Hickman, and at once discovered how he had been the victim of his credulity in gentlemanly, but indignant deportment.

HOW HE BEAT TWO BALTIMORE HOTELS.

Beau was instinctively a sportsman, and never missed attending the races. On one occasion whilst attending the Baltimore races he was fooled by his judgment, and bet too freely on the wrong horse, so that when the races were over he was out of money, and was compelled to resort to some clever dodges to maintain himself in Baltimore, and provide the

means of returning to Washington. His first dodge
was to procure his meals, and it was necessary, to
maintain his character for gentility that he should
affect the first-class house of that city. His first
attempt was at the B— hotel, where he enquired of
the clerk "if a gentleman could get meals for his
money;" to which the clerk very blandly replied in
the affirmative. Bean at once entered the dining-
room, and after monopolizing the attention of the
servants and dining sumptuously, he returned to the
clerk and threw down a small piece of coin, about
one-fourth the amount of the bill, and turned to walk
away. "But," said the clerk, "this is not sufficient
to pay for your dinner." "Why, sir," replied Bean,
"that is all the money I have, and you assured me
that I should have my dinner for my money." Just
then the proprietor stepped in and recognizing Bean,
he comprehended the situation of affairs and offered
him five dollars to go down to the G— hotel and play
the same joke on his friend G—. Bean readily
acceded to the proposition, and went down and
secured a royal supper on the same terms. G—
also felt the ludicrousness of his situation, and fearing
that his friend would find out about his being so
cleverly sold by Bean Hickman, he gave him ten
dollars to go up and play the same on his friend B—.
The next day, when the two hotel proprietors met to

laugh at each other, they learned from each other's revelations how dearly they had paid for Beau Hickman's patronage.

HOW HE OFFERED TO PAY A HOTEL BILL.

In his earlier days Beau was very fond of visiting the various cities where he had acquired a reputation as a fashionable man of the world. He prided himself, too, on his intimacy with some of the wealthiest sporting men who made the rounds of the different cities, and frequently accompanied them as companion. He happened in New York city on one occasion where he was unavoidably detained some weeks. Finally, his hotel bill was presented to him and he found himself utterly unable to pay it. In his dilemma he sought out a very wealthy sporting friend and asked the loan of a thousand dollar bill for a few minutes, which he knew him to possess. His friend accommodated him and Beau presented the bill to the clerk with the request that he would change it and deduct the amount of his board. The sight of so large an amount of money in his possession made the clerk very obsequious, and as he had not sufficient money on hand to change the bill, Beau was requested to make himself very easy about the matter, which he very willingly did until an opportunity presented for him to imitate the wandering Arab by stealing away.

HOW HE PLAYED IT ON A CONDUCTOR.

The races being over and Beau not caring to remain longer in Baltimore, he began to bethink him how he could work his passage back to his old haunts around the Capital. Nothing daunted he entered the gentlemen's car of one of the trains of the Baltimore and Ohio Company, bound for Washington, and placing an old card under the band of his characteristic high white beaver, (which at that time was rather more dilapidated than was his wont,) and taking an inside seat near a window, took a careless survey of the surroundings. After the train had started, when he noticed the conductor enter the car for the purpose of taking up tickets, Beau thrust his head out of the window apparently interested in some passing sight. Whilst thus apparently engaged, the conductor tapped him upon his shoulder to call his attention. Beau jumped back suddenly as if greatly startled and knocked his hat off out of the window. When he was informed of the purpose of the conductor he became greatly enraged and insisted upon having the train stopped to recover his hat and ticket. He became so very threatening towards the conductor for so rudely accosting and frightening him, that the conductor became alarmed at his untoward conduct, and begged Beau's pardon, but could only conciliate him by allowing him a free passage and promising to replace his loss by purchasing him a new hat on their arrival at Washington, which promise he faithfully performed to Beau's entire satisfaction.

HOW HE OBTAINED A PAIR OF BOOTS.

On one occasion when Beau had become greatly in need of a pair of boots his inventive genius was taxed for the following ruse, which was adopted to procure the much needed pedestal casings: Hastily entering the shop of a fashionable artisan, he gave his order for a pair of boots, to be delivered at his rooms at a certain hour on the second day following. Having given his precautionary instructions that they should be delivered promptly at the hour named, he went to another shop and gave the same order and similar instructions.

On the day specified, at the precise hour, the first dealer sent the boots by a shop-boy. Beau drew the right boot on and pronounced it a capital fit, and then pretended to exert himself in trying to get the left one on, but apparently failed and gave it back to the boy to take back to his master for the purpose of having it stretched in the instep, charging the boy to be in haste, as he was just about leaving the city on a a protracted visit.

No sooner had the boy left, and he concealed the boot he had retained, than another boy from dealer number two entered with the pair of boots that had also been ordered. Beau tried on the left boot this time, and expressed himself much pleased with the fit, but when he tried the right boot he found the same objection, and very petulently dispatched the second boy back to his master with the right boot to be treated as had been ordered with the left one of the other pair.

Thus possessed of a pair of new boots he sauntered out of his apartment to enjoy a stroll in the fashionable quarter of the metropolis, and to meditate on the bootless meeting of the two shop-boys on their return at his closed doors, each having a boot that would mate the other, yet not being a mated pair.

HOW HE BREAKFASTED WITH A STRANGER.

As illustrative of his unscrupulous impudence in his efforts to husband his resources against contingent necessities, the following imposition was practiced upon an accidental acquaintance with whom he met one morning at a restaurant. During the course of the breakfast the restaurateur jovially introduced Beau as being one of the celebrities of the Capital.

Beau of course took advantage of this opportunity, and, by his apparently very anxious interest in the stranger, insinuated himself into a degree of confidential familiarity. The stranger having finished his meal asked the restaurateur the amount of his bill, when Beau very pleasantly remarked, as though half in jest, that if it was convenient he would take it kindly if he would just settle both bills together, and very blandly expressed the hope that, in case he proposed remaining some days in the city, he would have the pleasure of conducting him to some of the places of interest and amusement. The stranger very good humoredly took in the situation, and paid the reckoning for both. Afterwards, when he learned the true character of Beau, he would tell his friends the story of how he paid for his introduction to the celebrated Bummer.

HOW HE LIVED.

Sometimes, when away from Washington on a protracted visit, Beau would find it quite difficult to make all the "ends meet," and was sometimes compelled to resort to humiliating dodges to procure the necessary means to return to Washington. On an occasion of this kind, he happened in Baltimore, where some friend took up a collection by passing a hat around in a well filled bar-room for his benefit. The contributions were quite liberal, and the collection realized quite a handsome sum. Beau very thankfully received the money, and proposed that all present should take a drink, which they all very willingly consented to do. After drinking, Beau inquired whether all present had taken a drink, and being answered in the affirmative, he very coolly replied, " Well, that's all right, now let us all pay for our drinks like gentlemen," at the same time throwing a ten cent piece upon the counter as pay for his own drink. " But," remonstrated the party, "you invited us to drink." " Certainly," replied Beau, " but did not promise to pay for your drinks." " But you certainly cannot mean to treat us so shabbily," insisted the victimized party. " Why, that's the way I live," replied the incorrigible Bummer, and very politely bowed himself out of the saloon.

WHEN THE CABINET DINE.

Beau was very fond of entertaining strangers from the country and took great pleasure in gratifying their curiosity by good naturedly answering their questions, and apparently becoming interested in their proper understanding of everything about the capital city of the country. Sometimes he would amuse himself by indulging in a pleasant canard, or relieve the monotony of a prosy story by some amusing facetiousness. A stranger was once asking him concerning the habits of the great men of the country, and was curious to know of some of their domestic habits and customs. "At what hour do they usually dine?" inquired a stranger. Beau was amused at this curiosity, and entered into the explanation in detail, assigning to each of the Secretaries and members of the Cabinet a different hour until the night had been assigned away. "But when does the President dine?" inquired the anxious questioner. "Oh, he don't dine until the next day," was Beau's facetious reply, which seemed to be an entirely satisfactory arrangement to the stranger.

A JOKE.

It is said that when the fifty cent stamp was shown to Treasurer Spinner he detected the striking resemblance of the vignette to Beau Hickman, and to obviate any mistake he had engraved under the likeness: Samuel Dexter, Secretary of the Treasury. Beau is said to have insisted that the joke was rather fine, and claimed the benefit of the doubt.

BEAU AT THE CARNIVAL.

In the year 1871, when the wooden pavement was finished on Pennsylvania avenue, it was suggested by some of the live spirits of the city that the event was worthy of commemoration, and that it should be made the occasion of general rejoicing.

It was concluded that, inasmuch as it would be completed about the time when the annual carnivals are held in New Orleans and other southern cities, a similar celebration would be the best way to impress upon the mind of the public the importance of the occasion, as it was an interesting occasion not only to the people of Washington, but to the whole American people. Every one looks with pride on the Capital of his country, and every Washingtonian looks with pride on Pennsylvania avenue, the most beautiful boulevard in the city, and every way worthy to bear the name of that noble State, the Keystone of the Union. Perhaps no event in the history of Washington ever called together such a vast concourse of people as was assembled on that occasion, young and old, heads of families with their little ones, bewitching misses, sallow looking old maids and courtly bachelors, young gentlemen with mustaches waxed to agonizing tightness, nursing babies carried by their mothers, stuffed with paregoric and soothing syrup to still their cries, and in fact the whole population of the city, together with numerous visitors, bent on enjoying the pleasure the féte afforded.

Arrangements were made for races of every description—horse races, mule races, foot races, sack races, pig chases, dog chases, and in fact races and chases of every kind that would afford amusement. The most celebrated and valiant knights (for which the neighboring States are noted) were enlisted to tilt for the honor of crowning the Queen, and he who won that honor did it by his good lance, for the many thousands assembled would not have allowed anything but fair play. Hembold the Buchu man, with his celebrated team, together with all the famous teams in the country, were shown off on the avenue; but with all these attractions no card drew so well as Beau Hickman on his steed, which by the way was an old gray mare. "The boys" had rigged him in grand style, and he was the observed of all observers, for this was about the first time within the knowledge of the oldest inhabitant that Beau had been *seen* without an *ante*, and as his name was so well known throughout the country as the "Prince of Bummers," there was great anxiety to see him, and many were the inquiries as to which was Beau, and upon his appearance in the arena all eyes were bent upon him, and many were the gibes and jokes hurled at him, and right bravely did he bear them. He bestrode his gallant steed with all the dignity of a king, accepting with equanimity the jest or compliment, only regretting when the free-ride was over, although he was heard afterwards to remark that he was very sore, and it is alleged that he took his meals standing for some time afterwards.

On the second day Beau was the first to enter the arena and a loud shout of applause along the entire avenue welcomed him as the Momus of the occasion, and during his charges up and down the avenue he was cheered lustily, and received the plaudits with a characteristically graceful bow. He seemed to enjoy the carnival throughout with a dignified pleasure.

A BOOTBLACK'S STORY.

During the carnival a stranger asked a bootblack standing at the corner of Seventh street and Pennsylvania avenue, " Is that the renowned and celebrated Beau ?" " Yes, that is Colonel Beau Hickman, he has been putting on a good deal of style for the last two days, and intends to enter that pony for the trotting race." " How does he live, does he work ?" continued the stranger. "Oh no, he had a good deal of money left to him, but he spent it all in a very short time, and since has been living on the interest of the money he spent—so they say." This explanation was entirely

satisfactory, and the bootblack drowned his interrogator's last question by a loud applause at one of
Beau's faets of horsemanship.

ON THE WAY DOWN THE HILL OF LIFE.

From about the year 1856, Beau commenced going
to the "demnation bow-wows," as was his favorite
expression, at rather a youthful age. His early dissipation told heavily on his physical constitution, and
the leathery features began to grow in his facial
appearance, and the bunions and corns increased and
enlarged on his pedal extremities until he had the
appearance of an old man hobbling in his gait. His
fashionable dissipation and his peculiar mode of living
having worn out a life that might otherwise have lasted
a score of years longer. But with all his faults

HE WAS NEVER A DRUNKARD,

And during the last years of his life when invited
to drink by his friends he would step up to the bar
and claim either a cigar or ten cents, the cost of a
drink, which would always be cheerfully handed
him. Indeed, this habit has been regarded as
one of the best temperance lectures of the age, and
Beau's fortitude in resisting the temptation and refrain-
ing from becoming a common drunkard is only another

evidence of the order of character of which he was possessed, but failed to turn to a more useful account.

Beau and Bummer as he professed and prided himself, yet he possessed some admirable traits of character,

HE DESPISED A LIAR,

And, although he practiced many questionable "dodges," yet he was never known to wilfully tell a lie or make a promise which he would not perform.

If in his "bummings" any one at first denied having any "change," and afterwards offered to respond, he would indignantly decline to receive it upon the ground that a falsehood had been told, a circumstance that brought many a blush to more pretentious persons.

During the late war he had considerable luck with the officers quartered at and visiting the city, but he always bewailed the "unpleasantness," remarking that it was a serious injury to his profession, "For, you know," he would say, "these d——d yankees have not the same liberality of southern gentlemen." After the close of the war Beau began to decline rapidly, and could be seen hobbling about the hotels with seamed and leathery face, anxious to ply his profession, but he had outlived his time.

HOW HE PLAYED THE BARRISTER.

Beau's sympathy on one occasion for an old friend

who had been arrested for some trivial offense, was so highly wrought that he offered his services to appear for him before the city court. Mayor Lenox was then in office, and the offender was duly arraigned before him. Beau very gravely arose to put in the prisoner's defense, but was abruptly disposed of by the Mayor, who informed the assuming barrister that if he did not quit the court-room he would be sent to the workhouse. Beau immediately abandoned his client, and left him to the mercy of the Mayor.

Some time after the Mayor's term of office expired, Beau met him and reminded him of the interference with his practice, and said, "See here, Mayor, you are no longer in office, and I think we had better settle our account, its getting too large." The Mayor laughed good naturedly at Beau, and in accordance with the custom paid up back dues and all.

POOR BEAU.

He had already lived too long to sustain the eclät of his profession, and together with his failing spirits and physical infirmities he began a rapid decline, and was often snubbed by those who only knew of him in his decline and failures. But there was still a class of old residents surviving who knew him in his better days and recollected the brilliancy of his early career as sportsman and Beau, who still respected his "assessments." It was only a few days before his last illness that a wealthy resident met him hobbling along the streets and paid him his last assessment of ten dollars, more from force of habit of old time usage than as a charitable gratuity.

In the latter part of the month of August, 1873, he was suddenly stricken down with paralysis and sent to Providence Hospital, where he received the kindest attention from the good Sisters. He was unable to move or speak or make known his wants for some days. He thus unconsciously lingered until the first of September, when, on a calm Sabbath afternoon, he quietly breathed his last without a motion or moan. Thus passed away Washington's great celebrity, unhonored but not unknown; for, probably, no character was more proverbially famous than that of Beau Hickman, and, although the prestige of his career had waned, yet he retained his renown in the traditional history of the Capital.

His sudden death caused a sadness in the places of his old haunts, and elicited many a generous expression of sympathy; and many of the habitues of his old resorts felt like Prince Henry at the supposed death of Sir John Falstaff, that they "could have better spared a better man."

A TOUCHING INCIDENT

Occurred in the hospital when poor Beau was breathing the last of his life away, which caused the eyes of the Sisters and attendants to dim with sympathetic tears. A little five year old boy was laying on a pallet opposite the dying Beau, and hearing the physician announce his inevitably approaching end, the little fellow propped himself up and in all the innocence of boyish sympathy called to Sister Beatrice and said, "If poor Mr. Hickman dies put these flowers on his grave for me," at the same time handing her a bouquet of beautiful flowers which had been given him by some lady visitor.

That bouquet was preserved by the kind Sister and afterwards placed on the coffin as was requested.

His remains were interred in Potter's field at the expense of the corporation. No fashionable pageant —no weeping mourners followed his bier to the pauper's tomb. He died as he had lived, and the only token of affection that relieved the cold indifference at his death was the tear-damped flowers contributed by that little companion in Providence Hospital.

SHAMEFUL DESECRATION.

On the following day after the burial several of his friends who had not before heard of his death contributed a sum sufficient to give his remains more decent interment in the Congressional Cemetery. Hacks and carriages were furnished at the various hotels for the accommodation of all who wished to attend the second funeral, and thus give expression to their kindly remembrance of the famous celebrity who had so long contributed to their social enjoyment. Arrangements had been made for the disinterment of the remains, and when the grave had been opened the coffin was found broken open and the body most shamefully mutilated. The scalp had been removed from the cranium and the brains taken out, the heart removed and other inhuman mutilations to the body. The sight was as sickening as it was revolting to decency, and the last rites were hastily performed and the new grave closed up forever over the mortal remains of a most remarkable man, possessed in life of a character strangely compounded of all the idiosyncrasies of genius. Notorious in life, he left behind a name and character that will live for years as the most eccentric Bohemian of the age, and prince of American Bummers; and the sad catastrophe of his life will serve as a lesson of warning to the rising generations, that a life without some definite aim and worthy object must prove a sad and deplorable failure.

The following poem was contributed to the *Capital* newspaper at the time of Beau's death, and reflects the general appreciation of his harmless character and kindly remembrance of a common friend:

BEAU HICKMAN.

Beau Hickman had no friends, but he died without enemies.—
Evening Star.

His quarters for jesting hereafter,
  Will be pitched in the land of no mirth,
The jester who moved us to laughter
  At a quarter a piece upon earth.

But he'll shamble around and not mind it,
  In spite of his bunions and cramps;
Quaint business I reckon he'll find it,
  While dunning the angels for stamps.

He will pun on the key of St. Peter,
  And the trumpet of Gabr'el he'll toot,
And bore them in rhyme or in meter,
  And charge them a quarter to boot.

That is, if they charge him for lodging,
  But there they ne'er dicker or trade,
So Beau will be done with his dodging,
  Since the debt he owed nature is paid.

And his face that was tanned into leather,
　I suspect will its freshness regain,
For the airs of that beautiful weather
　Will woo away wrinkles and pain.

I have heard that Beau was dishonest,
　A statement I scorn to believe,
For he paid every cent *if he promised,*
　Doing neither he did not deceive.

He professed to subsist without labor,
　A wag and dead-beat it is true,
But they say he ne'er slandered his neighbor,
　Which is more than his neighbor can do.

Of his faults I have mentioned a sample,
　There were many and barren of love;
But the good I have written is ample
　To secure him a corner above.

And I bid him good night, without feeling,
　Poor Beau! with a vagueness of tears;
So stopped have the wheels of his being,
　And the weights have run down with his years

CENTENNIAL GUIDE

TO

WASHINGTON CITY AND VICINITY

THE CAPITOL.

The first and greatest object of interest to the visitor is the Capitol, a magnificent building, situated a little east of the centre of the city, and can be readily reached by the Pennsylvania Avenue, F street and Belt line of city railways.

The interior of the Capitol is grand; the Rotunda, which one naturally views first upon entering, is directly in the centre of the building, and is divided into eight panels, between which are four bas reliefs of historical subjects, representing respectively, "Preservation of Capt. Smith by Pocahontas," "Landing of the Pilgrims," "Conflict between Daniel Boone and Indians," and "Penn's Treaty with the Indians." The paintings occupy. ing the several panels are "Declaration of Independence,"

"Surrender of General Burgoyne," "Cornwallis' Surrender at Yorktown," "Washington's Resignation at Annapolis," Embarkation of the Pilgrims," "Landing of Columbus," "Baptism of Pocahontas," and "Discovery of the Mississippi by De Soto." A number of other paintings adorn the Rotunda; and the sculptor, too, has done his part in the embellishment of this part of the Capitol. These are but a few of the objects of interest which the visitor will find in the Capitol, and to which they will be conducted by the Police, whose duty it is to see to comfort of visitors, and to conduct, or direct them to such places of interest as they desire to go.

THE WHITE HOUSE.

The Presidential Mansion, known all over the country as "The White House," is on Pennsylvania Avenue, at a distance of over a mile west of the Capitol, and is within easy access by way of the Pennsylvania Avenue Street Railway cars, which run directly in front of the grounds. It is 170 feet front and has a depth of 86 feet, and is situated on a plot of ground comprising an area of 20 acres, and the building itself is on an elevation of 44 feet above the Potomac. On the opposite side of Pennsylvania Avenue, and in front of the Executive Mansion is Lafayette Square, which is beautifully ornamented with trees, shrubbery and flowers. This square contains the celebrated Equestrian Bronze Statue of Jackson, the work of Clark Mills, who has the honor of being the first artist to succeed in erecting a statue of a steed poised on his hind feet; cannon captured by Jackson in his conflicts with the British, constituted the material of which the statue was made; it cost $50.000. Nearly all parts of the Executive Mansion are accessible to visitors, and something of interest may be found in all of the apartments; but the east room is especially deserving of attention. This room is 80 feet long, 40 feet wide, 22 feet high, and is furnished with much splendor.

SOLDIERS' HOME.

On a high plateau three miles north of the Capitol is the Soldiers' Home or Military Asylum. The site was selected by General Scott, the object being the establishment of a home for the worn-out veterans of the United States Army. The main building is 593 feet long, and built of East Chester Marble. The drives leading to this retreat are exceedingly fine and romantic.

NATIONAL OBSERVATORY.

The National Observatory, which has already played a part in the world of science, was erected during the administration of President Tyler, and is situated between the President's House and Georgetown, at the distance of about a mile from the former. The building is two stories high, and surrounded by a a movable dome. The Equatorial, which is a fourteen foot refractor, is mounted in the revolving dome, and it is worth while to observe the splendid machinery attached to it. This Observatory lies in north latitude 38° 53′ 39″, and west longitude 77° 2′ 48″

from Greenwich, and is itself a meridian. This is one of the most interesting places to visit in the district, and visitors will always find some one in attendance to show and explain the objects to be seen.

INSANE ASYLUM.

The Insane Asylum which is built of brick and is 74 feet long, surrounded by highly ornamented grounds, and is situated on a prominent elevation in a retired spot on the east bank of the Potomac; the style of architecture is Gothic; embattled parapets surround the whole building, and while the facade presented is extremely simple, it is yet very rich. The institution is well conducted and is worthy a visit.

CONGRESSIONAL CEMETERY.

The Congressional Cemetery, originally called the Washington Parish Burial Ground, is beautifully situated on the eastern branch of the Potomac, about two miles from the Capitol. The grounds are laid out in splendid style, with paths and avenues running all around and through them. The remains of General Taylor, Henry Clay, John C. Calhoun, and others, whose names are historical, reposed for a while in the vault of this Cemetery. Here too are monuments in memory of Naval heroes, while the red men of the forest has representatives in various graves.

THE GOVERNMENT PRINTING OFFICE,

One of the largest establishments of the kind in the world, is located directly north of the Capitol. Nearly all the printing and binding required by Congress, and the numerous Government departments in Washington, is done in this building, and the most recent and perfect machinery is used in the execution of the work. A visit should not be omitted by the inquiring visitor.

––––––

WINDER'S BUILDING.

Northwest corner of F and 17th street. It is owned by the government and used for the accommodation of a variety of public officers, namely, the Chief Engineer of Army, the Battle Record Room, Judge Advocate General of the Army, a portion of the Adjutant General's Office, the Army Ordinance Office and Museum, and the Second Auditor of the Treasury.

––––––

METHOD OF NUMBERING STREETS, &c.

For one not familiar with streets, localities, and points of the compass in Washington, a reference to the map will be necessary to illustrate this explanation of the somewhat complex system of naming and numbering the streets, which has always been a source of confusion to the stranger. This system, however, when fully comprehended, enables one to find any given street and number without assistance.

The city is now divided into four sections, the Capitol being the centre, respectively denominated Northeast, Northwest, Southeast, Southwest. Streets of the same names appearing in all these sections, and the same avenues, in several cases, traversing more than one section, it is customary in stating an address to add to the street the initial letters (as N. E., etc.) of the section in which it is located. *An exception to this rule is the Northwest section, which contains the main portion of the city, regarding which the indicating initials are dropped, and by common usage it is understood, when no section is stated, this section is meant.*

The streets running east and west are lettered, and those running north and south are numbered, except some very short streets which intersect blocks.

The buildings are numbered upon the Philadelphia plan. On the lettered streets, running east and west, and lettering each way from the Capitol, and avenues running diagonally, the numbers of the buildings begin at North and South Capitol streets, and count each way, the numbers of the streets indicating hundreds, those between First and Second streets including from one hundred upward, between Second and Third streets from two hundred upward, and so on.

The numbered streets running north and south count each way from the Capitol, and the buildings thereon number from the dividing line, viz: The Government Reservation No. 2, on the west, and East Capitol Street on the east of the Capitol. The system of numbering is the same as with the lettered streets, the numbers being located to correspond with the letters of the alphabet.

TREASURY DEPARTMENT.

Pennsylvania Avenue and 15th street, east of the Executive Mansion. Visitors admitted daily, except Sunday, from 9 A. M. to 2 P. M.

With a written order from the Secretary, and under the direction of the Superintendent, the visitor can be admitted to the Printing Division of the National Currency Bureau.

NEW BUILDING FOR STATE, WAR, AND NAVY DEPARTMENTS.

To the west of Executive Mansion is now being erected the magnificent building which is to accommodate the State, War, and Navy Departments. It will be an imposing structure with four fronts and it is expected will surpass all other buildings in Washington except the Capitol.

THE WAR DEPARTMENT

Occupies the building on the west side of the Executive Mansion, and fronts Pennsylvania Avenue.

THE NAVY DEPARTMENT

Occupies the building a little south of, and similar in appearance to, the War Department edifice.

THE DEPARTMENT OF STATE

At present occupies a building belonging to the Protestant Orphan Asylum of Washington. The building is located on 14th street, and is temporarily occupied by the Department until the completion of the building mentioned in connection with the War and Navy Departments.

THE POST OFFICE DEPARTMENT

Is located on the square bounded by 7th and 8th, and E and F streets, about half way between the Capitol and Executive Mansion, and three squares north of Pennsylvania Avenue. This is the site of the first Post Office which was burnt in December, 1836. The present building is one of the finest structures in Washington. The architecture is Corinthian, and material white marble, which gives a beautiful and imposing effect. It has a front extending two hundred and four feet on E street, north, with wings of three hundred feet on 7th and 8th streets.

THE INTERIOR DEPARTMENT

Is located in the Patent Office Building. This magnificent structure, the object of which is so closely connected with mechanical and social progress, is in all respects admirably adapted to its purpose. The principal front, with its splendid portico, looks down 8th street.

THE DEPARTMENT OF AGRICULTURE

Occupies the building in the Mall, a short distance south of Pennsylvania Avenue, and between 12th and 14th streets. The beauty of its grounds and surroundings are equally attractive to the simply curious visitor as to the farmer, to the admirer of the beautiful as to the botanist.

SMITHSONIAN INSTITUTION,

The fine grounds and building of this Institution are in the Mall or Government Reservation No. 2, facing Pennsylvania

Avenue and opposite South 10th street, west. The surrounding grounds directly attached to the building cover twenty acres, and with the remainder of the reservation, are under Congressional control.

The founder of this Institution was James Smithson, an English gentleman, son of the first Duke of Northumberland, a native of London, and a graduate of Oxford, who died in Italy in 1828.

The National Museum is the most interesting feature of the Institution. It contains the specimens gathered by more than fifty exploring expeditions of the Government from every quarter of the globe.

THE DEPARTMENT OF JUSTICE

Is presided over by the Attorney General of the United States, and is accommodated in the south wing of the Treasury Department Building.

The tall shaft of marble west of the Department of Agriculture, and so distinctly seen from all parts of the city, is the unfinished

WASHINGTON MONUMENT,

The corner-stone of which was laid July 4, 1848. The original design contemplates a circular building 250 feet in diameter and 100 feet high, and above this an obelisk seventy feet square at the base and 500 feet high.

THE ARSENAL

Is located on the extreme southern limit of the city, at the mouth of the Eastern Branch, and is in full view from the Navy Yard. Curiosities from the battle-fields in the late war form a feature of special interest.

ORDNANCE MUSEUM

Is in Winder's Building, northwest corner of F and 17th streets. This museum contains many objects of great interest, namely, the captured confederate flags, specimens of uniform and equipments, models and drawings, curious arms of many kinds, ages, nationalities, and sizes.

ARMY MEDICAL MUSEUM,

And office of the Surgeon General of the United States Army, is located on 10th street between E and F streets, in a building which was originally a church, subsequently Ford's Theatre, and specially interesting as the place of the assassination of President Lincoln.

THE COAST SURVEY OFFICE,

Under the care of the Navy Department, is in a neat and commodious building on Capitol Hill, and within a few steps of the southern entrance to the Capitol grounds.

MOUNT VERNON.

Mount Vernon belongs to the people of the United States. By contribntion they purchased it, and they have full control over it. It is eight miles below Washington, and occupies one of the most beautiful and romantic sites to be found on the banks of the Potomac. Its great attraction is, however, to be found in the fact that it was the home of Washington, and that his honored remains there quietly repose. There Washington lived and died, and there he and his wife quietly sleep. Mount Vernon has therefore become the Mecca to which Americans annually make pilgrimages. Among the objects of interest are pictures of the Washington family, the key of the Bastile, presented to Washington by Lafayette and others. The lid of Washington's white marble Sarcophagus is wrought with the arms of his country, and has simply inscribed upon it the one name, "Washington."

Steamer Arrow, Captain Frank Hollingshead, leaves foot of Seventh street at 10 o'clock daily, Sundays excepted, for Mount Vernon.

THE CONGRESSIONAL CONSERVATORY,

Where rare plants from all parts of the world can be seen in full bloom, is opposite the west side of the Capitol grounds and south of Pennsylvania avenue. There are several thousands specimens in the collection, arranged in different conservatories, according to the required temperature.

CORCORAN ART GALLERY.

Mr. W. W. Corcoran, a wealthy citizen of Washington and a liberal patron of art, has erected a beautiful building with all the necessary appointments for a complete art gallery, entirely at his own cost, which he has donated to public uses and conveyed to a board of trustees to be held as a perpetual trust. It stands at the northeast corner of 17th street and Pennsylvania avenue. It was commenced in 1859, and in 1861, when nearly completed, was taken by the Government for the use of the Quartermaster's Department, and surrendered to its owner in 1869, after which it was finished and dedicated to its intended purpose.

Open daily from 10 A. M. until near sunset; free on Tuesdays, Thursdays and Saturdays. Admission, twenty-five cents, on Mondays, Wednesdays and Fridays.

THE NAVY YARD,

Located in the eastern section of the city, on the Anacostia
River (the eastern branch of the Potomac.) The grounds
comprise about three hundred and fifty seven acres, and are
approached, on the land side, through a handsome gateway,
contiguous to which are several guns, trophies of naval
warfare, the inscription on each stating its history. The
workshops, ordnance stores, mementos of maritime adventure, ship-houses, and frequently monitors and war vessels,
present objects of interest sufficient to occupy very profitably
the time of the visitor. Near the yard are the Marine
Barracks and Marine Hospital.

YOUNG MEN'S CHRISTIAN ASSOCIATION

Have a handsome building at the corner of Ninth and D streets, where the stranger will always find a welcome. The rooms are open from nine A. M. to ten P. M. Newspapers and magazines, religious and secular, from all parts of the country, are to be found in the reading-rooms. The library embraces about twenty thousand volumes, of nearly every class of literature, and is free to all to read in the rooms; and by the payment of an annual fee of two dollars, books can be taken away. The membership fee, entitling to all the privileges of the Association is four dollars annually.

www.ingramcontent.com/pod-product-compliance
Lightning Source LLC
Chambersburg PA
CBHW031242260626
47169CB00007B/2412